Drawing Really Cute Baby Animals
With lowercase letters

Created By **STEVE HARPSTER**

HARPTOONS
PUBLISHING

WWW.HARPTOONS.COM

This book is dedicated to my wife Karen, who told me again
and again to do a drawing book using lowercase letters.
(You were right.)

WWW.HARPTOONS.COM

Library of Congress Cataloging-in-Publication Data
Library of Congress Control Number: 2010902904
Harpster, Steve

Drawing Really Cute Baby Animals With Lowercase Letters
written and illustrated by Steve Harpster

SUMMARY: Learn how to draw cartoon baby animals
         using lowercase letters a through z

   ART / General, JUVENILE FICTION / General

ISBN 0-615-59572-3
ISBN 978-0-615-59572-6

SAN: 859-6921

Printed in the United States of America by Bookmasters,
Inc. 30 Amberwood Parkway, Ashland, OH 44805
JOB # 50002122
Date of production- February 2nd 2014

Want Steve Harpster to visit your school and draw with your students?
Email steve@harptoons.com for more information or visit www.harptoons.com.

WARNING: These pages are full of super cute, cuddly little animal babies. Long exposure to this many cute animals may cause permanent smiling, joyful singing, and the occasional kissy-face while saying "Coochie coochie coo." **Enter at your own risk!**

Andy the alligator

Basil the bunny

Cooper the orca

Dougy the puppy

Erin the chick

Frannie Fish

Gertie the elephant

Herbie the porcupine

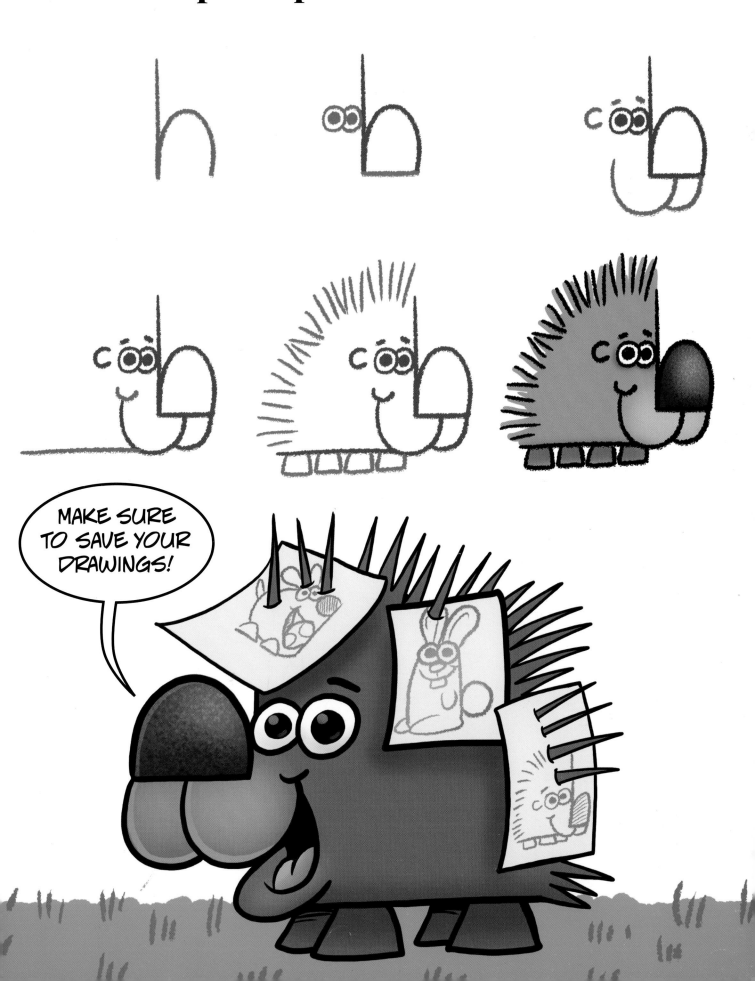

Izzy the lemming

Jasper the seal

Monty the snake

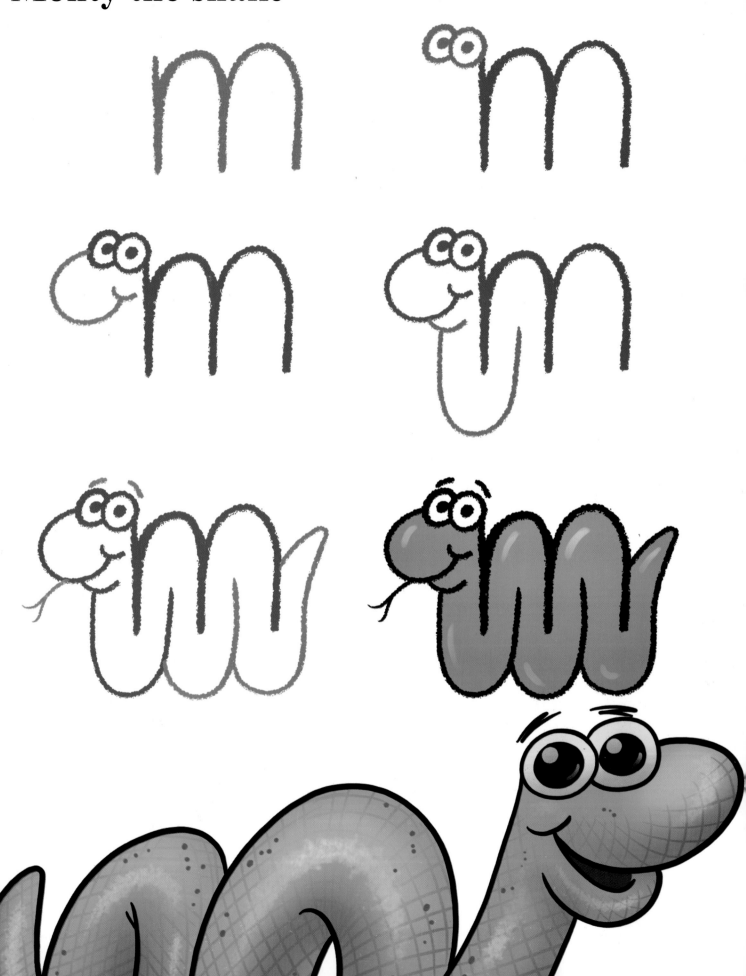

Nate the chameleon

Opal the bear

Petey the turtle

Quimby the duckling

Rascal the squirrel

Tyler the aardvark

Uggy the gopher

Vinnie the hedgehog

Willie the goat

Xara the pony

Yuri the lion cub

Zachary the joey

About Steve Harpster
Steve Harpster lives in Cincinnati, Ohio with his wife Karen and two boys, Tyler and Cooper. Harpster visits schools all over the world teaching students how to draw animals, monsters, and cartoons characters using numbers and letters.

Other drawing books by Steve Harpster

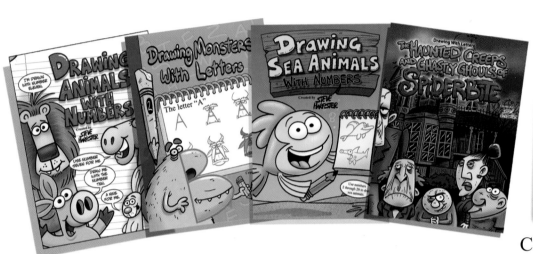

Coming in Spring 2014
**Drawing Dragons
With Numbers**

Learn to Draw at
WWW.HARPTOONS.COM

• Watch how to draw videos

• Download activity pages

• Free drawing/coloring pages

• Find out how to have Steve Harpster visit your school online or in person

• And much, much more